Dear Parent:
Your child's love of reading starts here:

Every child learns to read in a different way and at his or her own speed. Some go back and forth between reading levels and read favorite books again and again. Others read through each level in order. You can help your young reader improve and become more confident by encouraging his or her own interests and abilities. From books your child reads with you to the first books he or she reads alone, there are I Can Read Books for every stage of reading:

SHARED READING
Basic language, word repetition, and whimsical illustrations, ideal for sharing with your emergent reader

BEGINNING READING
Short sentences, familiar words, and simple concepts for children eager to read on their own

READING WITH HELP
Engaging stories, longer sentences, and language play for developing readers

READING ALONE
Complex plots, challenging vocabulary, and high-interest topics for the independent reader

I Can Read Books have introduced children to the joy of reading since 1957. Featuring award-winning authors and illustrators and a fabulous cast of beloved characters, I Can Read Books set the standard for beginning readers.

A lifetime of discovery begins with the magical words "I Can Read!"

Visit www.icanread.com for information
on enriching your child's reading experience.

For my parents, who
gave me a choice of three
names just like Gigi.
—M.I.

I Can Read® and I Can Read Book® are trademarks of HarperCollins Publishers.

Gigi and Ojiji: What's in a Name?
Copyright © 2023 by Melissa Iwai.
All rights reserved. Printed in the United States of America.
No part of this book may be used or reproduced in any manner whatsoever without written permission except in the case of brief quotations embodied in critical articles and reviews. For information address HarperCollins Children's Books, a division of HarperCollins Publishers, 195 Broadway, New York, NY 10007.
www.icanread.com

Library of Congress Control Number: 2022943659
ISBN 978-0-06-320809-4 (hardcover) — ISBN 978-0-06-320808-7 (pbk.)

Book design by Chrisila Maida and Stephanie Hays

22 23 24 25 26   LB   10 9 8 7 6 5 4 3 2 1   ❖   First Edition

GIGI AND OJIJI

WHAT'S IN A NAME?

GERALDINE

MELISSA IWAI

HARPER
An Imprint of HarperCollinsPublishers

"These pancakes are the best!" said Gigi.

"Are they as good as Roscoe's?" asked Mom.

"What?" said Ojiji, Gigi's Japanese grandpa.

He was confused.

Roscoe was the dog!

"Mom means Roscoe's Diner," said Gigi.

"When we first got Roscoe,

he didn't have a name," Mom said.

"We went to Roscoe's Diner," said Gigi.

"I got the idea for the perfect name!"

"He's been Roscoe ever since," said Dad.

That made Gigi think of her name.

Her parents named her Geraldine.

She also had a middle name.

It was Hanako.

"Why am I called Gigi?" Gigi asked.

"You couldn't say Geraldine," mom said.

"It was too hard for you back then."

"That means Gigi is a baby name!" said Gigi.

"I want to be Geraldine from now on!"

"Okay," said Mom.

"Okay, Geraldine," said Dad.

"Ge-ral-dine . . ." said Ojiji slowly.

It was hard for him to say it!

After breakfast, Gigi decided to draw Roscoe.

Gigi loved to draw.

Ojiji did too.

Gigi always signed every picture.

"Geraldine is a long name!" said Gigi.

"My hand is getting tired."

"Hanako is shorter," said Ojiji.

"It's even shorter in Japanese!"

"Can you teach me?" asked Gigi.

"Hai!" said Ojiji.

Gigi knew hai meant yes in Japanese.

Ojiji showed Gigi how to write Hanako.

Hana means flower.

Ko means child.

Writing in Japanese was like drawing!

"I will be Hanako from now on!" said Gigi.

"Hai!" said Mom and Dad.

"It is easier than Ge-ral-dine," said Ojiji.

Later Gigi said, "Can we go to the library?"

"Good idea!" said Mom.

"We have books to return."

"Don't forget your library card, Hanako!"

"Huh?" said Gigi.

Then she giggled.

She forgot she was Hanako now!

Gigi loved the library.

Choosing new books was the best!

"Welcome back, Gigi!" said Ms. Lee.

Ms. Lee was the librarian.

"I'm Hanako now!" said Gigi.

"Is that a fact?" said Ms. Lee.

"Do you want a new library card?"

16

Gigi didn't answer right away.

"Um . . ." she said.

"Why don't you think about it?"
Mom said.

"There's no rush," said Ms. Lee.

"I know I'll see you again soon!"

After lunch, Gigi said, "Let's play catch!"

"Hanako!" yelled Ojiji.
"Look out!"

BONK!

It was too late.

"Dai jou bu?" said Ojiji.

Gigi knew that meant "Are you okay?"

"Hai," she said rubbing her head.

"We're so sorry!" said the Frisbee players.

"Let's go get ice cream," said Mom.

It was busy at the ice cream parlor.

Ojiji went to place their order.

Mom looked at Gigi's head.

Luckily, Gigi wasn't hurt.

"I heard Ojiji try to warn you," said Mom.

"I didn't know he meant me!" said Gigi.

"But you said you are Hanako now,"
said Mom.

"I know," said Gigi.

"But I don't feel like it's me.

What do I do?

Ojiji likes the name Hanako," Gigi sai

"And it's easy for him to say."

CLASSIC FLAVOR

- French Vanilla
- Chocolate
- Strawberry
- Cookies ___ ___eam

- Mint-n-Chip
- Salted Caram___
- Rocky Road
- Pistachio

"Hanako is a nice middle name," said Mom.

"Then what will Ojiji call me?" asked Gigi.

Gigi thought about her name again.

Geraldine was too long!

Hanako was not her.

Maybe the perfect name was . . .

"GIGI!" a woman called.

"Order for Gigi!"

"That's me!" said Gigi.

"I heard what you were saying," said Ojiji.

"I put the order in your name.

I think Gigi is the perfect name

for you," said Ojiji.

Gigi agreed.

She would be Gigi from now on!